I'll Be Your Friend, Smudge!

For Rebecca and Nina
M.M.

For Josh
L.C.

ISBN 0-439-60726-4

Text copyright © 2001 by Miriam Moss.
Illustrations copyright © 2001 by Lynne Chapman.
All rights reserved.
Published by Scholastic Inc., 557 Broadway, New York, NY 10012,
by arrangement with Gullane™ Children's Books.
SCHOLASTIC and associated logos are trademarks
and/or registered trademarks of Scholastic Inc.

12 11 10 9 8 7 6 5 4 3 2   4 5 6 7 8 9/0

Printed in the U.S.A.   40

First Scholastic printing, February 2004

I'll Be Your Friend, Smudge!

Miriam Moss
Illustrated by Lynne Chapman

SCHOLASTIC INC.

New York   Toronto   London   Auckland   Sydney
Mexico City   New Delhi   Hong Kong   Buenos Aires

Smudge yawned herself awake in her new room in her new house. Stripe poked his head round the door. "How many days till my birthday?" asked Smudge. "One less than yesterday," replied Stripe, as he did every morning.

Suddenly Smudge sat up. "Then it's today!" she cried, jumping out of bed. "Happy Birthday!" smiled Stripe, handing Smudge her present. It was a beautiful box of paints.

Downstairs, Smudge painted while Stripe cooked a delicious birthday breakfast. Suddenly Smudge put down her brush, looking worried.

"Who will come to my party?" she asked.
"I don't know anyone who lives around here."
"You'll soon make some friends," said Stripe,
"but we could have a special party this year,
just you and me."
Smudge tried to look pleased.
Quickly, Stripe added, "Perhaps we
could build a treehouse to have it in!"
Smudge's face lit up.

All morning, Smudge and Stripe worked hard.
Smudge drew plans of the treehouse while Stripe
sawed and hammered. By the afternoon the house
was built. Stripe went to find a rug for the floor.

Smudge sat in the treehouse, waiting for Stripe. However hard she tried, she couldn't help feeling sad that she had no friends to play with on her birthday. A tear spilled on the ground, splosh! Then another, splosh! Then another, splosh! splosh!

Suddenly something moved below.

"Well, bother me, it's raining," said a voice.
Smudge peered down. Two bright eyes stared back.
"Hello," said Hare, climbing quickly up
the ladder. "I'm Hare, who are you?"
"Smudge," replied Smudge.
"What a lovely treehouse!"
remarked Hare.
"Is it yours?"

"Yes," said Smudge, wiping her eyes.
Hare looked at her more closely.
"Why are you crying?" he asked.
"We've just moved house *and* it's my birthday
and I haven't got any friends to come to my party,"
Smudge said, all in a rush.
"I'll be your friend," said Hare. "And I've got
some other friends you can meet too. Come on!"

"Hello, Stripe, this is Hare, he's going to be my friend and he's got some other friends I can have too! Can we go and find them in my boat?" asked Smudge. "Of course," smiled Stripe. "Why don't you ask them to come and play in your new treehouse."

As they rowed off,
Hare spotted Goose.
"Upside down as
usual," remarked Hare.
"Hey, Goose! Turn
down-side-up!"
Goose popped up, her
mouth full of river weed.
"This is Smudge,"
said Hare.

"Hello, Fudge,"
said Goose.
"*Smudge*, not Fudge,"
corrected Hare.
"It's her birthday
and this is her boat.
She's got a treehouse
and we're all going
back there to play,"
said Hare. "Come on!"

Goose followed Smudge and Hare.
"Goose, have you seen Mole?" Hare called.
But before she could answer, a nose appeared
from an earthy volcano on the bank.
"Oh, look, there he is!" Hare cried.

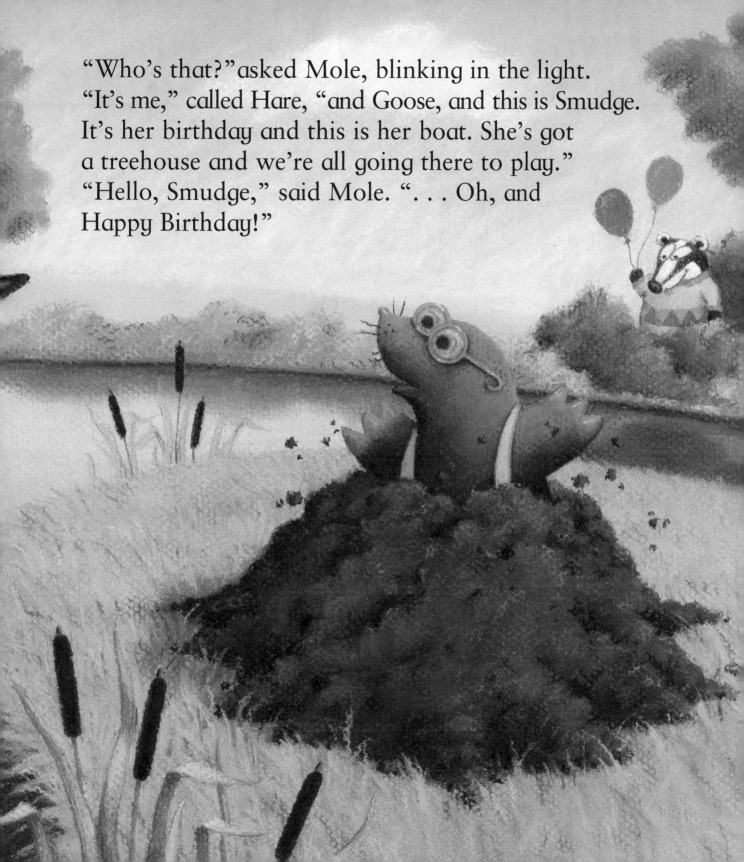

"Who's that?" asked Mole, blinking in the light.
"It's me," called Hare, "and Goose, and this is Smudge.
It's her birthday and this is her boat. She's got
a treehouse and we're all going there to play."
"Hello, Smudge," said Mole. ". . . Oh, and
Happy Birthday!"

"Climb in, Mole!" said Hare.
"Oh no," said Mole. "I'm afraid
that boat is far too wobbly for me."
"Don't worry," said Hare. "You can
sit between us."
"It will still wobble, Hare," worried Mole.
"I promise, it will hardly wobble at all,"
insisted Hare.

At last Mole was persuaded to climb in
and the new friends set off for the treehouse.
"Race you down river, Goose!" shouted Hare.

They had almost reached the bank, when **Thunk!** Goose
bumped into the boat and the three friends flew backwards.
"You're all down-side-up!" Goose remarked.
"Oh, Goose!" laughed Hare, "You forgot to slow down!"

Poor Mole was wobbling like a jelly.
"Are you all right, Mole?" asked Smudge,
offering him a hand.
"I think so," said Mole, pushing his
glasses back on. But when he saw the
treehouse, Mole felt much better!

Inside the treehouse, Stripe had laid out a delicious tea. There was even a birthday cake in the shape of a paint box!

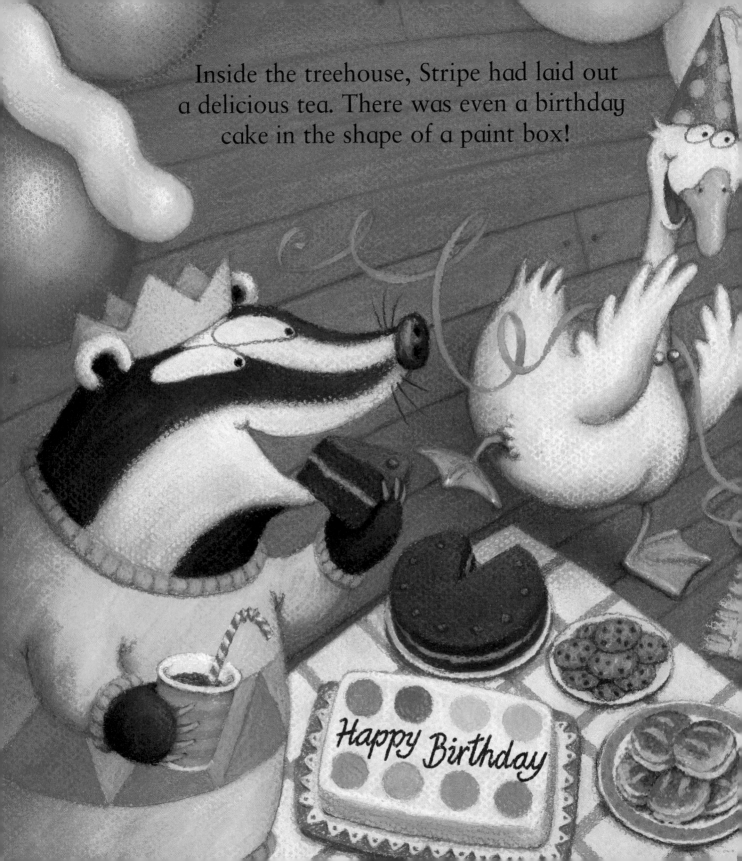

The new friends sang *Happy Birthday*
to Smudge, ate their tea and played games
until it was nearly dark.

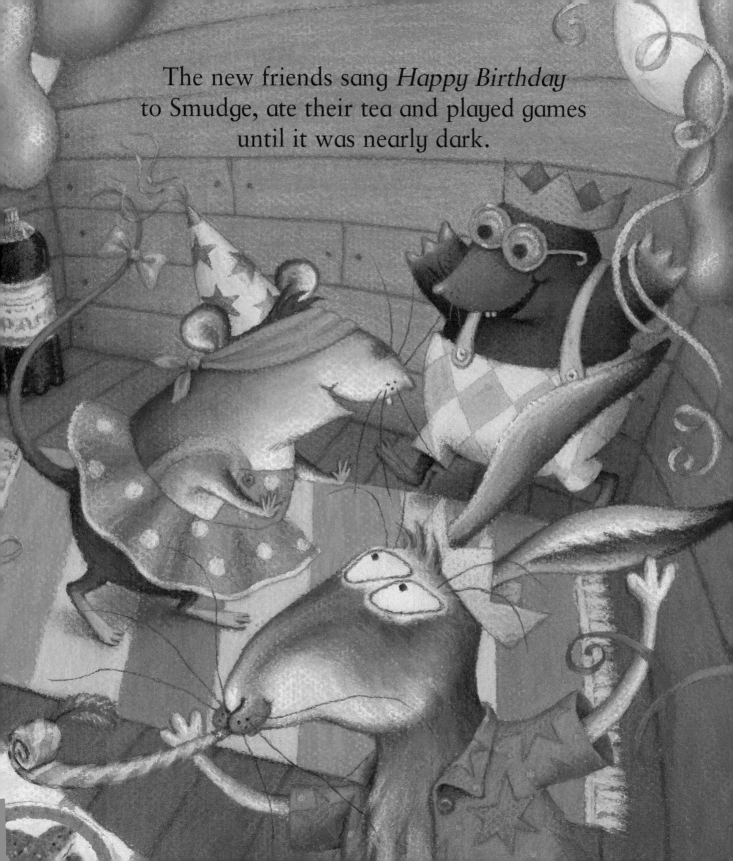

That night, Stripe tucked a very happy Smudge into bed.
"Did you have a nice day with your
new friends?" asked Stripe.

But there was no answer.
Smudge was fast asleep.